MURDER in *Lavender*

JULIA GRAZIANO

978-1-965552-15-5 (Paperback)
978-1-965552-08-7 (e-book)

admin@bookwrightshouse.com
☎ (213) 286 6700

Chapter One

"Oh, it's you!"

"Well yes, I remember being invited or do I have it wrong," said Michael.

"No, your right I just didn't expect you to be so early. I'm the one that's always early; it's kind of my thing."

"Your thing, I don't understand"

"Well, it is a long story, replied Ayden.

"But I would like to hear it, and we do have some time, answered Michael.

"Ok, but no laughing. When I was in high school there was a group of girls who picked on everyone, for any reason. I had them in some of the clubs I belonged to and any sport teams. They always found a way to make you feel small. They would pick on you if you were late, even a minute. I made sure that I would always be early. I just didn't want them picking on me and humiliating me. I guess it just stayed with me, so I am never late for anything". Ayden felt her cheeks getting red, she was blushing. She never felt like this before and wasn't sure she liked. For the last year she had put all her time into her work. She never thought of getting to know any one especially a man. She just didn't have time for romance. She had seen Michael most mornings but didn't have time to stop and have any long conversations, it was always just a quick hello.

"But I'm so happy that you came, I wasn't sure you would."

"I have been seeing you every week for almost a year trying to find a way to get to know you better, of course I had to come. I'm so grateful you asked me, I never have the nerve to ask, I'm always afraid of being rejected.

"And I wanted to get to know you better too, so this worked out great." said Ayden. "I hope the Egyptian Display it worth our time. It has had great revues and I just love this kind of thing; you can't believe the ideas I get from some of the clothing or jewels. So, shall we go in?"

"Yes, let us begin our exploration of all things Egyptian. Please explain what we are looking at though. I really do not know anything about the Egyptians, even though I remember having to study something about them in school."

Chapter Two

"So my darling, how do you feel," he asked in a soft whisper?

"Oh, I feel so good; it's never been this good".

So, you now see the benefit of having your ankles and wrists tied to the bed with the softest ribbon. It is all about pleasure my darling."

"And pleasure was sure what it was," she replied slightly out of breath.

"You just rest a moment, and then we have more fun."

He climbed off the bed and took a swallow out of the bottle they brought with them from the bar they were at earlier, the one where he found her. That was one of her great faults, she always picked up some stranger and brought them home. Ayden told her time and time again that one day she would pick up the wrong man and she would be sorry.

He made himself irresistible to her. He removed a small plastic bag from his coat pocket and pulled off his latex gloves and put them into the bag and sealed it. He then proceeded to pull on a clean pair from his other pocket, put them on and laughed. "American women, so gullible and trusting, you tell them you have a terrible case of Poison Ivy that you caught helping your poor frail mother to plant some flowers in her little garden and so need the gloves so she wouldn't get any and she believes you. Even a trained nurse, doesn't want to see how bad it is and if she can do anything to help him.

"Yes, stupid and trusting, this is even too easy for me."

He gets back on the bed and kisses her and immediately her nipples start to firm.

"Do you want me to undo the ribbons yet, we still have much more pleasuring to do."

"No," she replied.

"Alright then let us get to the best part."

He removed a small knife from under the pillow that she never even felt. Straddling her he turns her face to himself and kissed her again and told her that the pleasuring would begin. He grabbed her jaw making her mouth open and very quickly stuffed a folded cloth handkerchief into it. Then he fashioned a bow with the remaining ribbon he had and tied it around her mouth.

"Now where to begin, oh yes I think these nice long legs first, don't you agree?"

With the small extremely sharp little knife he began to cut her on her left leg causing small lines that quickly filled with her blood. Being so deadly drunk she didn't even move at first.

"Now I have practiced long and hard to make this beautiful, only one inch between cuts. Like this and like this, and soon he was up to her entire leg. It finally caused some moaning in her, but he just ignored it and began the same exact lines on her right leg. Then he preceded the same practice on her arms. By this time she felt the stinging and tried to pull herself free but as she pulled the ribbons around her wrists they just got tighter. She turned her head back and forth trying to get the handkerchief out of her mouth but it was so well tided in.

He continued slicing around her neck and down her midsection. Now he sat back looking at what he had just done. I have done a good job he said to himself, but I must finish and be away soon. Now what is left to do? He rembered her nipples the way when touched they would harden and stand up straight, so he tried touching them and got the response he desired.

"We are almost done my darling," he whispered to her, but by now she had passed out. He held one nipple, squeezed it slightly and proceeded to slice it off, then he did the same with the other one.

"One more thing to do," he said to himself again.

He drew more of the lines around her face. Then two large crosses from her forehead to jaw.

"Then he said to her, "now to put a smile on your face." He cut her from the corners of her mouth almost to her ears. Her jaw dropped. Then with his knife he stabbed her over and over into her chest. He was satisfied that she was dead, but something was missing. He didn't feel as though the job was done. It needs something more so maybe the other bitch would get the message. He looked around the room and saw a small lamp in the end table; he removed the shade and unplugged it. He then shoved it up inside her as hard as he could then pressed hard where he thought the bulb would be listening for the glass crushing. One last thing to make it complete and he took his knife sliced deep along her abdomen to disembowel her. Now he was done. He carefully removed the gloves putting them in the plastic bag, took a fresh pair and put them on, dressed and left the building. No one was out currently for it was only five thirty in the morning. He thought he saw a woman walking a small dog, but they were too far away to see him. He got into his car and slowly pulled out on to the road and drove away leaving his host to slowly bleed to death.

"A very good night," he said to himself out loud.

Chapter Three

"Good grief, look at this rain, I never even heard it in the display room, did You."

"No," replied Michael

"What are we going to do; we don't have any place to run to without getting soaked."

"No, you're quite right, unless Jeremy has a solution. Let me call him, if I know Jeremy, he is parked very close to the building. "Yes, I know it's raining smart guy, we were hoping you had any ideas as to our next move. No, I think dinner is out of the question considering the circumstances. Do you think you can see well enough to make it around the block, it's a one way down and the next is a one way up, let us off at my apartment house and we can all go in to get dry. What do you think? Good, now we just have to get to the car. No, stay there, I'm sure she can run faster then either one of us," continued Michael.

"Well do you think you can make it to the car?" Asked Michael. "Jeremy could run up with an umbrella, but I told him that you could probable run faster then either of us, so run it is. Are you ready?"

Before Michael finished his sentence Ayden was already off and running. Jeremy was there ready with an umbrella and the car door open. Ayden launched herself inside and moved over for Michael. Boy, I know one man out of condition she said to herself as she continued waiting.

"Come on, move it she yelled to Michael," who was huffing and puffing as he finally reached the car.

"I know someone who needs to hit the gym now and then, all that sitting you do every day is not helping your health." she tried to say without hurting his feelings.

"Yes, I know. Jeremy has been trying to get me to go with him, but I never seem to find the time," replied Michael." Since I can barely breathe, it is obvious I very much need to find the time, sooner then later. While you seem to run like an antelope, I feel I'm forever to be the tortuous", he said laughingly.

Jeremy with all his special skills got thru the rain, down the block, up the next and as if someone special was watching, saved him a parking place right in the front of Michael's building.

"How wonderful, a parking space right in front," said Michael.

"Come along Jeremy, I think I even have a six pack in the fridge with your name on it,"

"That is a fine offer Mr. D, but I am basically still on duty and as such have all the things I need in the trunk. Change of clothes, protein bars, fruit, pillow and blanket, everything I need."

"But you'll be chilled to the bone man. Why settle for this when a perfectly good abode awaits you." answered Michael.

"You know we pride ourselves on being prepared for anything, Mr. D that's why you use us right."

"Yes, you are quite right." replied Michael. "I have never once in the five years I have employed you and your company that I have ever been afraid for my well being,"

"Thank you, Mr. D., It means a lot coming from you"

"Well, if you change your mind or need something, any thing at all just come up and knock, loudly I might add since I sleep like a rock."

Since Jeremy could not be persuaded to join them Michael and Ayden scooted out the door and up the three steps to the main lobby. Shaking themselves off as the walked to the elevator, Ayden couldn't help but bust out laughing.

"You know a few more minutes in that rain in that wool suit and I really don't see you would be moving at all,"

"Oh, very funny, what do you weigh 100 pounds soak and wet? But you're right these wool suits must hold a gallon of water; I really do need to get to the gym. An accountant might be a good job, but it does make you sedentary far to long, and then there is my mother's Sunday dinners she won't let me out of, and you see the results."

Once inside Michael got them big towels for drying off.

"We need to get you out of those wet things," said Michael. "Don't suppose you were once a seal and came prepare with every thing Jeremy has." Laughed Michael.

"No, just a one-time Girl Scout and we usually just carry enough to makes' mores,"

"Ah, just the thing, wonderfully warm fire and long sticks for your marshmallow, graham crackers and a chocolate bar what could be better." said Michael.

"Sounds like you knew a few girl scouts," laughed Ayden.

"Yes, that was the thing, the girls learned to entice the boys to come over. Every Saturday night some one would have a fire in the back yard and all the boys would gather round waiting for our little sweet pieces of dripping chocolate and marshmallows. I think the parents liked the arrangement too. That way they always knew where we were, so we never could get into trouble. Children of immigrant parents were held so tightly to our parents, we could never do anything, but what do we do about you? I can give you a set of my pajamas, but you will need a belt or some thing to keep them up. Perhaps mother has something in her room; yes, I remember buying her a set a robe and nightgown. I had this especially decorated for her thinking she might come and spend a few days with me occasionally, but hasn't happened yet, and I've been here about four years already."

Michael looked in all the drawers and the closet and managed to come up with a long flannel night gown and matching robe and as luck would have it just a little larger than Ayden would wear.

"Tags still on them from a Christmas past, but I think they would do nicely."

"I can't wear your mothers Christmas present she never wore herself." said Ayden.

"You most certainly can, and you will if I have to call mama to get her permission."

"Alright, I give".

Ayden once in the guest room stripped off her wet things a fast as she could. She gently opened the package Michael took from the closet. It was so beautifully wrapped, but she had to open it. What she found was a beautiful set of matching nightgown and robe, embroidered with his mother's name. Quickly to the bathroom to wash off the grim on her legs in the shower, towel dried her hair which curled even more so. Oh, that warm water felt good, back into the shower she went to warm her body again with the warm water. It felt so good, she dried off and slipped into the nightgown, not really too, too large but certainly long enough, took out the robe and put it on, nice fabric, this was an expensive night set, too bad his mother didn't appreciate her gift, it obviously cost a few dollars. Adjusting the robe over the night gown and securing the waist with the matching tie belt she felt so much better, a pair of socks would make this wonderful outfit, cozy and warm. She opened the other drawers but found no socks. She quickly cleaned up the bathroom, hung the towels over the shower rod and walked out into the living room where Michael already sat.

"Michael, do you have any white socks, my feet are freezing," she asked.

"As a matter of fact, I think I do." He disappeared into his bedroom and returned with a brand-new package of white socks the wrap still on them.

"Wait, don't tell me your mother bought these for you one Christmas and you have never even opened them," said Ayden.

"Right you are, I think mothers are out of touch with the white socks given at Christmas as if I were still a little boy. That was the gift I received every year when I was a child, I sometimes think she hasn't noticed I've grown into adulthood," replied Michael with a somewhat sad look on his face.

"Maybe she does but, having you now as an adult takes away all those wonderful memories she had when you were a young boy."

"I supposed you could look at it that way. We didn't have much but there was always fun in the house at Holidays. No, I take that back, mama always made daily life good, she baked her own bread, made her own pasta and once a week she baked a cake or cookies, or some thing papa liked. She tried to make life good for us as best as she could."

"Would it sadden you to relive your childhood, I'd would love to hear how it was when they first came here, and how they managed," asked Ayden.

"No, it wouldn't, I haven't though of those days in so long I'm not sure I remember too much of it, but I know it was hard for all of them. Are you sure you want to hear about them?"

"Yes, I would, but one thing I would like to know first. Why does Jeremy call you Mr. D.?"

"It's kind of a joke, he knows my name is D'lane, but he also knows that I had my name legally changed when I was eighteen. Papa agreed when I told him that I needed to because people were still getting used to immigrants with the ethnic and sometimes hard to pronounce names and that it may be hard for me to gain employment. He understood having had the problem himself getting some of his jobs. Until he established himself as the best stone worker he also had some problems."

"So what is or was your real name," asked Ayden.

"Michael Umberto D'elansandro, How's that for a name to go through the day with," said Michael.

"Yeah, that would be kind of tough, but you were so lucky that your parents agreed, replied Ayden.

"Well mama said no, but papa made her understand it was for the best for my future and she finally came around."

"How long do you think this rain will continue, "said Michael?"

"Well, I haven't heard of anyone building an ark soon, so I think we have plenty of time and it would give us time to get to know each other better. I really know nothing about you, so you can explain how you grew up and how we are what made us who we are today. You tell me your story and I'll tell you mine another time."

"Alright but how about a nice hot cup of tea first," asked Michael.

"That would be wonderful, any thing I can help with? "No, I can handle the tea part but if you can find a blue metal round cookie tin, there may still be some of her sesame cookies she baked for me last week. I try not to open them when I get one; I feed the birds out on the roof. If I ate all the goodies, she makes for me I'd be twice as large as I am. She doesn't make it easy, always making some thing for me to take home after our Sunday dinners together.

She tries so hard, poor dear, her apartment is right over a bakery, and she could very easily get something from there instead of doing it herself."

"Yes, she could, but it wouldn't be the same, she's making you something out of love, who wouldn't rather have that. I would love to have some one do that for me what she does for you."

"You have a mother, doesn't she do that kind of thing?"

"No sad to say, let me help so I can see where things go, looks like I may be here awhile if it's all right with you, I think I told you that other then work I really can't say I know any one that I'm really close to.

"Ayden began to cry, she didn't like crying in front of anyone before, she was a private person and didn't like showing her emotions in front of anyone. A good part of growing up taught her to keep her emotions well hidden. Crying made her feel weak and never again would she let herself feel that way.

With hot tea and sesame cookies, she couldn't wait for Michael to remember the story of his immigrant parents as they made their way from Italy.

Chapter Four

Michael asked Ayden if she would prefer a teacup or mug.

"Oh, a mug if you have one, teacups are for those little old ladies and how they drink. Trying to show a bit of class they wished they had. I grew up with a mug and a mug I'll die with thank you very much."

"That's what I guessed but I thought I'd better ask first," said Michael.

"Oh, you don't think I can eat at a fancy place and use the proper silverware." she replied.

"I'm not getting into this with you, I'm afraid it's a battle I won't win," he laughed.

"You're right, you won't. Ok I'm nicely warmed up and ready for my story, wait, there is one thing I must know. Ayden had been holding this question for the entire day and knew sooner or later she would finally get to ask it.

"You dress like a lawyer all custom-made three-piece suits, winter and summer weight. Italian leather shoes, you walk and speak like a lawyer, you know all the best classier restaurants' you're on phone speaking to every person in a foreign country. I'm curious why you aren't a lawyer".

"Well if you'll be patient, you will find out in my story you insist I tell."

"I'm sorry; I promise I will sit here sipping my tea and listen quietly." she answered.

"I doubt that" he laughed. But he took a chance and began.

Chapter Five

"Mama and Papa came from the same village outside of Naples. They knew each other since they were children and as they grew, they knew they were meant for each other. Of course, their parents didn't know, they wouldn't have approved. Papa's family were fishing people and Mama's were high on the hill with livestock, mamas' family made their own pasta and sold it plus they baked fresh breads daily which made them more like royalty. They would meet silently and make plans. As soon as Mama turned sixteen, they would marry and take the boat to America. They saved every dime they made for their trip, another few months and Mama would be sixteen, and they could marry.

All went well, they married, had money they each saved plus money given to them by the families for setting up their house. Their parents still didn't know what they were about to do. They weren't alone, another pair was doing the same thing and they were so happy they wouldn't be alone when they reached America.

The trip seemed to take forever, but they finally reached their home as they began to call it. On the long trip, they got together and made out the plans they should do first. Get registered so they would be legal and could have papers so they could work. Then they had to find housing. Getting a house was way too much for them, even an apartment was too costly, so they did what others were doing. They rented an apartment with two bedrooms until they could save enough for their own place. Papa knew he could find work easily because he was a master marble cuter, but the other man was just a laborer and would have to seek out work every day.

It didn't take long for Mama and Papa to be able to afford their own place.

They felt guilty leaving but as chance would have it another couple was looking to find a place to share, and Papa put them together and everything worked out right. Mama was so happy, she tried not to get pregnant until they had their own place and just like magic it happened the first days they were in the apartment. Nine months later I was born. They haggled over my name; Mama wanted an Italian but Papa wanted an American name so I would fit right in as I got older. Finally, they agreed and so they chose Michael.. Papa said I could go any where with a name like that."

"What were your fathers name and your mothers?" asked Ayden.

"Your typical Italian name if you lived there, Father was Anthony James and Mothers was Anna Marie. You see typical, I bet half the village had those same names. I really can't imagine trying to communicate with each other when everyone was called the same, I guess that's why Father was so adamant about naming me," replied Michael.

"Ok where was I, Papa worked very hard to keep me in Catholic school he felt they were better, and as the last year came and we began to look over college, there was nothing I could say. I wanted to go to Fordham to become a lawyer; it was something I had dreamed about all my senior days. Sometimes when Papa went to look at a new job, he would bring me along and when he saw hard, cruel men in fancy suits, I saw something different, Class and power, this was what I thought made you an American.

We didn't even visit any colleges, Papa said NYU and I was going to be an Account. That was the first time I can remember arguing with him, I walked out slamming the door jumped down the stairs and out on the street with Papa yelling out the window. "You better be here for dinner your mother makes with love for you or you get none tonight". "I walked around for awhile, sat with the boys from some of the other families, some of whom were having the same problems. When I saw the time, I hurried home, I felt so bad having that fight with my father, I had to make up for it by giving him a chance for each of us to tell our reasons for our choices." Papa was waiting at the top of the stairs for me. "I knew you would be back; we never had such a fight, and we must act like men and talk to each other. Mama yelled not till dinner is over."

"Papa spoke first, then I realized there would be no conversation, what Papa said was going to be the way it was going to be and I had no say. Papa said he worked day and some nights for enough money to allow me to go to college and it was not to be used for some big time showing. We were immigrants, but we would become the best Americans we could be." I was disappointed but made the best of it, I took as many classes as I thought I could handle and by the third year received my diploma. Mama and Papa were more excited than I had ever seen them. Papa even took a few days off from work and took us to Coney Island. Mama loved it there, the sea breeze, the boardwalk, all the strange food. It was the best few days; I was happy with my Mother and Father." "How about more tea, it must be cold by now?"

"Yes, thank you Michael, but do you have anything stronger like brandy or something. I don't usually drink, but my insides feel cold, said Ayden?"

Chapter Six

"Yes, I think I do, a present from a client. Since I never touch the stuff, it isn't even open", he replied. "Yes, here it is, I hope it is something palatable. I am strictly a beer man myself, maybe that's were this extra belly is from." He and Ayden both laughed, He got down a small glass and started to pour, "Say when he said"

"Yes, enough" she said. "As tired as I feel you'll be picking me up off the floor."

"I think we should call around and see if anyone is still delivering, I hadn't realized it was so late, that's why you are probably so tired." Michael grabbed a handful of take-out menus and handed a few to Ayden. "Find something you like, and we will call around." Michael called a few places, but no one was delivering because of the severe downpour still going on outside. Michael's last chance was the little Chinese place less then a half block away. He hung up the phone, did a little dance and proclaimed all is well.

"They never fail to be very good, the food as well as their delivery service. I asked them to double the order in case we are still stuck here in the morning, because I know there is absolutely nothing edible in this kitchen. The woman who did the decorating added everything in case you wanted to, but I don't think heating up some Chinese soup cooking is really what she had in mind."

Michael rose and put the kettle on the flame. He checked the cupboards for anything they could eat and found a box with a few cookies. No telling how long these were in there, but dunking might soften them.

Michael parted the curtains to look outside and saw that it was raining so hard he could barely read the signs.

"Wow, come see this. It' like a freaky storm, I've never seen it rain like this before."

Ayden got up to look out the window.

"You're right, it's like a hurricane or something. I hope Jeremy is alright in the car. He's such a dope. Oh, I'm a trained seal and we're prepared for anything. Well, I hope he is prepared for this, it looks like it could go on all night.

"I'm sure he's fine."

The food came in no time, and each filled their plates, gobbled down half of what was on their plates, sat back, sigh, got up to stretch.

"That was such quick service for the amount of food that's here," said Ayden.

Michael added that the extra twenty he gave the delivery boy would make sure they would always get good service. Michael laughed and commented that in case they were stuck in again he would have enough to keep her fed.

"Are you implying that I eat a lot," she said.

"I imply nothing, I only tell the truth".

"Oh, I didn't realize how hungry I was," said Ayden.

"That's why I ordered double," Michael laughed.

"Ok mister, continue please, you wanted to be a lawyer but your father had other plans for you.

Michael just shrugged his shoulders and made his way to the much softer armchair.

Michael sat comfortably in the chair, took a sip of tea, and smiled at her.

"OK, begin", laughed Ayden.

"Are you sure this is what you want, there are so many things we could talk about that would be more interesting?"

"I'm sure," replied Ayden.

"Alright, if you insist.

"Most of the men were stone workers, brick layers, carvers of specialty work like my father, skyscrapers, banks and churches were going up and so eventually everyone was making some more money finally they had their own apartments, and Little Italy was born.

Mama said that father worked such long hours she barely saw him but each day she would rise, make his lunch and make sure he had a good breakfast. They started buying furniture a little at a time, my dad was extremely tight with money, he saved much more then he spent, but they finally had a place to invite friends most of whom came over with them at the same time on the ship.

Father's work was so good he had people who would only use him for the finest work. His name circulated quickly, and he always had plenty of work. Mama finally had me and the extra money was there for all things babies needed. I don't know, I don't remember those days.

"You jerk, if you didn't, I would really think there was something wrong with you, she laughed. How about some more tea, this is just getting to the good part."

With a new cup of hot tea, Michael began again.

Chapter Seven

"I made my communion and confirmation in the church that ran the school, I graduated when I was only sixteen, when my father had a day off, we always went to a museum or someplace educational, My father never did any thing for fun except go to Coney Island which was my mother's favorite thing to do. She loved to walk the boardwalk and get fried potatoes or ice cream. Dad always thought of educational things first. He never had a formal education and knew he was going to make sure I did."

"But what was it like at home, did your mom cook or bake special things, I was brought up by my mother as a single parent, well almost a single parent, we lived with my aunt and uncle at the bar and restaurant they bought to get out of the city. My uncle hated the city. We always had the best food, pasta every Sunday, Fish every Friday, eggplant parmesan sandwiches on Wednesday, even fried bologna, my Aunt Josie could really cook, I guess that's why the restaurant was always packed at dinner time."

Ayden dropped a cookie into her tea retrieved it and it was still hard. "I guess these have been around a while. Ok Mister continue please, you wanted to be a lawyer but your father had other plans."

"Yes, and I was so shocked I cried and I don't think I've cried since." He had hoped seeing all the pompous, arrogant men parading around in their flashy three piece suits and screaming at the workmen, he thought it would make my mind up for me. But it didn't. I told him I still wanted to become a lawyer. I've never heard my father yell like he did.

"No, no, no you will be what I tell you to be, and we will have no more discussion about it."

"But father we have had no discussion about it at all, shouldn't we discuss the matter before we decide."

"No, I decide, no lawyer for you, I have worked many years for those people, and they are thieves, crooked like a tree, trying to shorten men of the wage they agreed on before the job and then trying not to pay them their worth. No, these men are evil. This life is not one I want for my son." his father stared at him coldly.

"Then what do you have for me to do?' asked Michael.

"You my son will be an account, all I have met are honorable, and you work all day then have the weekends off to spend time with your family like I could not spend with mine. No this is what I want for you and beside; you will get full scholarship because of all your high grades. I would have to work many more hard jobs to keep you in a school like that, I don't think I can do it any longer, I'm sorry. I have never let you down have I?, now do this for me and your Mama who has also saved all she could to make sure you always had the best."

Having ended his story he turned to Ayden, "what would you have done if you were in my place," he asked.

"Well with such extreme parental authority, there would be nothing else you could do unfortunately," she replied. "Considering all they went through for you; it would surely break their hearts for you to turn your back on them now. I know if I had parents like that I would never go against them unless it was so incredibly important that you couldn't do any thing else But you know how much they did for you, you could always go back to school anytime and get your proper classes, pass the bar and you would both have what you want. But you would have to work as an account while getting your other classes. You father did so much for you; he needed to see you working as the best account. He wanted for you to be recognized as the best as he was in his field."

"Yes, I suppose your right," replied Michael. "Well, it is getting very late, let us clean up and head off to bed. Think you could get some sleep now" "Yes, I'm more tired than I thought, must have been the food," answered Ayden.

Chapter Eight

Ayden awoke with the smell of fresh coffee and bread, I must still be sleeping she thought to herself. The smell seemed to get better and better. She put on the robe, brushed her teeth, brushed out her curly red hair and cleaned up the bathroom. She opened the door and definitely smelled coffee. Michael was in the kitchen putting some bagels and pastries on a platter. Bringing it to the table he said,"Well up finally, I thought would have to knock and wake you."

"Where did this come from, have a friend at the pastry shop to?" "No" replied Michael "It was down to a sprinkle so I ran across the street to get this and just made it back when the skies opened up again. I don't remember when I've seen such rain. I put the weather report on and we were right to order extra food. They said it was a freak storm that might last another day or more." So get comphy, have some coffee, a bagel and go back to bed If you like, there's little we can do about it for now."

"Do you think Jeremy is alright" asked Ayden?

"Yes, he is fine, I tried his mobile and some time in early morning the rain let up and he managed to make it home. I guess seals are well trained."

Ayden drank her coffee ate a bagel with cream cheese and felt more tired then she did before. Michael saw her looking exhausted and gathered her by her shoulders and marched her towards her bedroom. Removing the cup she still held, he opened the door, pushed her in the room and told her not to come out until she felt like a human being. Ayden stumbled towards the bed, said goodnight and thanked him for everything he did.

"Goodnight Michael" she said.

Michael didn't have the heart to tell her it was nearly eleven o'clock, there was nothing she could do, and he already had the table cleaned. H grabbed a paper while he was out and sat at his desk to see what was going on around the world. "Well, nothing good, just like the days before". But something good did happen, he got to spend time with the girl in the office that he had seen so many times but barely spoke to. He found her such a delight, not like so many of the women from the city, she was fun.

Ayden finally rose again "coffee, coffee, me need coffee", she mimicked the monster from Frankinstein.

"And are you lucky," said Michael "I just put on a new pot, and it should be ready in five minutes, giving you enough time to tame that hair that seems to go where ever it wants to."

"Oh, the hair, it does have a mind of its own, to bad you don't have this, then I could laugh at you. She stuck her tongue at him and walked back to the bedroom. With no will power she knew she could sleep for the rest of the day, but when she saw the time, she hurried. She couldn't believe it was nearly four o'clock. She just had breakfast and in another two hours she will have dinner. "I hope Michael got some sleep, he looks great," she thought.

Chapter Nine

Just at that moment the phone rang, Michael got up to answer it.

"Yes, yes, not extremely well, but I do know her roommate better. Yes, I know exactly where she is. Because of the storm, she stayed over in my guest room until I could get her home. May I know what this is about?" Michael listen for a while then said, I think my driver could get us to her apartment; the rain seems to have let up some. May I ask how you got my number? Yes, I understand. Are you sure you need us to leave now, it will be very dark soon. No, we will be there as quickly as we can, yes thank you.

Michael hung up then phone then picked it up again, "Jeremy, Michael here. I just got a very strange call from a Detective"

He said he was in Brooklyn and needed us there now. Do you think we can make it in this rain?

"I'm sure, I'll be there in twenty minutes, get dressed as fast as you can. Did you tell Ayden, he asked".

No, I knew she would have questions and I didn't have any answers, he replied.

"Ok, see you soon".

"Ayden stop what you're doing please. I just received a call from a Detective in Brooklyn at your apartment. I don't have any answers for what's going on, just that he wants us there as soon as we can so, please get dressed, Jeremy will be here in twenty minutes."

Chapter Ten

It had stopped raining and Jeremy knew all the short cuts to get them to Ayden's apartment. "Standing outside was a man who looked like a cop. Michael opened the door all the while Ayden was behind him.

"Keep her in the car, I don't want her seeing this, the Detective yelled to Michael, ask your driver if he has a way to lock the doors so she will stay put. Jeremy nodded his head and pushed a select button that locked all the doors. Ayden was yelling at him.

"Sorry sweets be patient, and all will be revealed".

"I hate this, treated like damn kid, if it's my apartment then I should be allowed in."

The Detective introduced himself as Detective Steve Hildebrant, as he and Michael shook hands.

The Detective asked Michael if he knew Ayden's roomates. And did he ever see a dead body.

"Don't knew her that well, but I think I could recognize her alive or dead."

Good I hope you have a strong stomach for this, most of my guys heeved brought it up a few times already, that's why there is a bucket out in the hallway. He described it as the worst he has ever seen. As he led Michael, he could hear Ayden yelling. As he followed the Detective inside, the smell from all the vomit produces such a strong smell, his mind started racing, what did he agree too?

The Detective led him inside and into Ayden's roommate apartment. There lying on the bed ankles and wrists tied to the ends of the bed. Michael felt his stomach getting ready to throw up, but he didn't want to embarrass himself even after he was told some cops heaved all ready, he held it in. What Michael saw was as grotesque as you can imagine cuts everywhere on her body. In the middle of her chest was stab wounds from a much larger knife Michael agreed it was Betty Thomson on the bed and had to exit the room holding a white handkerchief over his mouth Ayden couldn't stay still, she pounded the doors trying to get out of the car they locked her in.

"Jeremy let me out Michael looks sick".

"Michael is fine and will be here soon".

Michael composed himself and headed for the car. Jeremy unlocked the doors and Ayden couldn't wait for the door to open completely and jumped from the car.

"Are you all right she said to him as she had him by the lapels of his jacket," "What's going on, they had me locked in this car, I need to know what don't they want me to see, is Betty alright? Michael, please tell me what they wanted?"

Michael got himself into the car without all the antics of Ayden.

"I will tell you all if you will just calm down", Michael replied. You could see that Michael was deeply disturbed.

"Hey, how about a cup of coffee," said Jeremy. "it got chilly sitting in the car and there is one right around the block"

"Yes", said Michael, "coffee sounds good right now."

Jeremy began to move the car, but Ayden was anything but patient.

"Please tell me what the hell is going on".

Michael responded in a very calm voice that if she waited without all the antics and allow him to have his coffee, all would be revealed. That was not the response she wanted but it was better then none, besides she could use some coffee, she was chilled to the bone. Upon entering the diner, they took a booth in the back and ordered three coffees. Michael wriggled out of his coat and took a sip of coffee. Ayden let him relax for a moment, she was sure he would tell her everything, Michael was the most honest person she ever met.

<h1 style="text-align:center">Chapter Eleven</h1>

"Michael began by telling them that it was the most grotesque thing that he had ever witnesses. Ayden prepare your self for the worst. I will not sugar coat it for you. Are you ready for this?"

"I'm ready; just tell me the truth, leaving nothing out."

Michael began telling them what he saw even as tears came from his eyes. His body shook relating every thing Ayden needed to know. She asked him a dozen questions about the situation. Michael answered her trying to stay on track. When he finished summing up his story, Ayden asked to be let out of the booth. Michael let her out and was surprised when she opened the door to the diner and went outside even though it was cold.

"What is she doing", asked Michael as he watched Ayden just stand there at the end of the block. She didn't move, just stood there.

"Should I go get her? asked Michael.

"No", said Jeremy, "She is probably compartmentalizing everything, she'll be back when she's done."

Michael had to ask Jeremy what the hell he was talking about, he should get her before she freezes. But as he started to get up Ayden came in sat down and ordered three hot cups of coffee and two slices of apple pie warmed.

Michael asked what she was doing, and she replied very casually that she was having pie with her coffee. A slice for her and they would have to share the other pieces or order their own. The pie and coffee came, and she devoured it as if she hadn't had a meal in days. Then adjusted her coffee the way she liked it and slowly sipped it.

"Christ you are the most exasperating woman I have ever met", said Michael. Jeremy sat comfortably on his side of the booth and just laughed at the two of them.

"Michael, relax everything is fine, now eat your pie or I will." Michael picked up the pie plate and put it on top of hers, and she ate it like she never had pie before. Michael got up and paced the floor. Jeremy just shook his head.

"Had to compartmentalize everything, didn't you"? asked Jeremy. "That's good; we learned that in the Seals, I don't know how many times it saved my life. Michael just doesn't understand the process, just give him some time, he's a good man just watching over you, this was pretty horrible, and most people would cave under such a thing. He doesn't know just how strong you are".

Michael wouldn't look at Ayden, just said that they were expected at the station in half an hour. Michael paid the bill, left a healthy tip and left the diner and got into the car. Ayden followed and didn't talk to him, just slide on to the seat where Michael had moved further into the car. Jeremy started the car and tried to remember where the station was. He rounded the block then the other and said damn it I thought it was here somewhere here.

Ayden coolly said that it was two blocks down and hang a right and they would be there, and she was right.

Detective Hildebrandt was pacing back and forth in front of the door and finally stopped when he saw the car pull up.

"I thought I gave you the wrong address," he said.

"No, no, Ayden had to have something in her stomach, she is like an alligator, she can eat any thing and at any time even after she just heard the most horrible details about Betty, I don't know how she does it."

"Well let's just go inside and get this over with, Betty's parents are coming soon, and I think it would be better if you were gone by then," said the Detective. He ushered them to a desk and ask to speak to Ayden alone first.

Chapter Twelve

Where did they meet? What did they do together, did they have other friends they spent time with together.

Etc, etc, etc all the same questions you see them ask on police shows. Ayden was so bored.

"Look I have answered all your questions," said Ayden, "there is nothing else I can tell you."

"I'm sorry Miss Ayden I know this is hard for you especially since it is about your roommate, but it really is important," replied the Detective, "and we are almost near the end, are you sure you can't think of any thing else we may have missed."

"I'm sure I have said everything," said Ayden biting her lip. "No, no there is something else; I'm not sure how important it is but sometimes the smallest thing could be important right."

"Yes, yes, your right, what do you remember." said the Detective.

"Mr. and Mrs. Thompson and I were going to ask Betty to leave the apartment by the end of the week because of her drinking and bringing men home after work. They would be up all hours of the night making one hell of a racket and it really upset the Thompsons. She was fine when she first moved in but then started going crazy with the men. I even had to put extra door locks on my bedroom door because sometimes they would be trying to pull it open, I even put locks on the windows. One night I had to run to the bathroom and there was Betty and her latest buck-naked swing each other down the hall, or on there hands and knees biting each other any where they could reach, it was gross. They would carry on until early in the morning until Betty fell asleep and the guy would quietly creep out. She always picked up one of the men at the little bar she walked to on her way home when her shift was over. They would park their car up by the tree, No one really ever saw them except Mrs. Thompson because she walks the dog around five or six just when they would be leaving, Mrs. Thompson would knock on the door to tell me they had just left and we would go into Betty's apartment and make sure all the candles were out, Betty always had candles burning, and was always naked with a bottle of whiskey still in her hand. This happened at least twice a week depending on her shift. So that is why we wanted her out. Watching some stranger pea all the way around the hallway was more then we could take."

"Did you know any of them," he asked.

"No, I didn't, I thought I recognized the color of a suit one of the men was wearing but I wasn't sure, I see a lot of different colors of fabric where I work, but I couldn't be sure, but it was a strange purple tone color, maybe Dimitri might remember, he remembers almost every color out there. Well that is all I know, I'm sorry I can't remember anymore," Said Ayden.

"No, you have helped us a great deal, thank you very much. Now please send one of the gentlemen in."

It didn't take long for Jeremy and Michael to be interviewed, neither of them knew Betty very long, and after everything I told them about her, they were very glad. They were all exhausted and it was getting late.

Chapter Thirteen

Michael and Jeremy were each given a chance to tell the Detective what they knew about Betty, which was not very much, but Detective Hildebrant was satisfied with what he got. He thanked them all for everything, handed them each a card and asked them all to try and remember any thing else and if they do, please give contact him. He thanked them again and asked them to stay in touch if they remember anything more. He told them that Mr. and Mrs. Thompson would be coming in and he hoped that they would meet with them and maybe together they might recall some thing more. Ayden said she did plan to see them and hopefully they would remember more. She thanked him and they left "Well that wasn't too bad," said Ayden. "I just wish that I took more of an interest in Betty's life, maybe I would have more information. Hopefully Annie new more since they spent more time together, especially at the bar drinking." Ayden didn't like wasting her time at the bar; she didn't like drinking with a bunch of strangers.

"Thank heaven you weren't at that bar and at that night. It could have been you lying dead, and I would never got to know you, sorry to put it so bluntly, said Michael."

"Sorry Ayden but I have to agree with Michael", well it has been a long night, how about dinner," said Jeremy.

"That's great if you can find a place that has enough food for Ayden," laughed Michael.

With dinner over, Jeremy drove them home said goodnight and said he hoped he had to hear no more about murder.

Ayden hated to ask Jeremy but somehow found the strength.

"Betty's parents are having a small memorial for Betty" said Ayden. The men all sighed but Ayden knew they would go, at least for Ayden's sake. The memorial was short and the Thompsons were so grateful, there were many friends of theirs and it was good for them too, Mrs. Thompson pulled Ayden aside and thanked her for all she did taking care of Betty and she wanted her to know that she and her husband agreed to give her plenty of time to fine a knew place and that they were not holding her to the rent she gave them for the two months she paid before she moved in. Ayden could feel the tears on her face as they ran down.

Ayden thanked her and told her that she would stay in touch and gave her the business card with her cell number on back.

"Thank you for everything, and if you need anything don't hesitate to call her then quickly said goodbye". She knew the guys came because of her and she was so grateful, so she wanted to leave for them. You could see the relief on their faces when she told them she was ready to go.

Jeremy sighed and "yelled food, food, food." everyone laughed at him but all agreed. "Nothing fancy," said Ayden. "I'm too tired to eat heavily this late". Michael agreed.

"How about that little diner, Ayden seemed to like that apple pie" Jeremy laughed.

"That's good enough for me," said Ayden.

Chapter Fourteen

Ayden could barely eat a thing which was most unusual she was just feeling so guilty, her head says one thing, but her heart says another. She put her PJ's on and fell fast asleep. It was Michael's idea that she stay at his apartment for a few days until the police told them she could return, not that she wanted to, she never wanted to live in that place again. Nightmares and dreams were her entire night, twisting and turning, in the morning she could barely drag herself out of bed. One thing she kept remembering was the day she was working late to put the final touches on the drawings of her new spring line but kept getting annoyed by the flashes of light she kept seeing out of the corner of her eye. She finally decided to go and find out where they were coming from. No one should be in Dimitri's office; he was not in the building. A man was in there with a camara taking pictures of some of the drawings.

"Hey who are you and what are you doing" yelled Ayden.

The man grabbed his camera and pushed Ayden aside and ran out the door. Ayden caught herself from falling and ran after the man. He was small, about Ayden's height and was wearing a suit and hat that he had pulled down to cover his face. Ayden couldn't place him, but she recognized the suit, it had that funny color that looked red and lavender at the same time. She knew that fabric from somewhere but couldn't remember where. At work the next day she told Dimitri, but he said to just forget the whole thing, and he didn't photograph any thing important because she had the new designs. Ayden did as Dimitri said and tried to forget it, but there it was in her dreams. It must mean something she told herself, but what?

She finally got dressed and she decided not to go to work which was another decision go to work or don't go to work. Children made decisions so easy, yes or no. She remembered how easy it was then, Mom would ask if she would like to do something today and YES or NO came out. To bad it still wasn't that easy. She decided to look for something for breakfast. There was absolutely nothing in the kitchen to eat? She was about to put her coat on and find some place to eat when Jeremy knocked and let himself in. "What are you doing here?" she asked. "I thought the boss would have you driving a million miles today because he missed a few days," asked Ayden.

"Nope, my orders for the day are to spend it with you, doing whatever you want to do. Michael didn't think you would want to go to work today, I don't know how he does it "but he usually is right. So where to"?

"Oh, Jeremy it's so glad to see you, I was just putting my coat on, and you know there isn't a thing to eat in this house, I think we should go shopping for food and junk food, what do you think"?

"Anything you want said the boss, so let's fine some food" replied Jeremy.

"The little grocer around the corner should have most of what we need, Michael knows I'm not a very good cook unless you are very fond of grilled cheese."

"Michael doesn't have to eat much during the week, his Mama cooks for him on Sundays" replied Jeremy.

"I was there on Sunday, I thought she was cooking for the army, we brought some home and I think that it is the only edible thing to eat. It's no wonder Michael is caring a little extra pounds. I know his grandfather and his father died quite young, he really needs to do something, the gym or something just a walk around the block, I said that I would even go with him but nothing, not even a ho hum.

"Oh, lets us get some greens and things then he would have to eat, I know he wouldn't like letting me have dinner alone, laughed Ayden."

The two of them wandered thru a few stores and finally the little grocer. The two of them strained carrying their loads. They got to their building and put everything down, putting freezer food in one bag, refrigerator in another bag and the rest could remain on the counter in case the wanted to go out again. The elevator came down and after everyone got off. Ayden jumped in with the bag full of freezer veggies and ice cream. "Just want to get this in the freezer, you can get the next one, ok", she said.

Just as Ayden was unlocking the door, a strong arm suddenly went around her neck. She fought and fought but who ever this was he was very strong.

"Finally; got you this time bitch." said the voice.

"Ayden asked what he wanted and why was he was calling her "bitch," as far as she knew she had never done any thing to him to warrant this treatment and besides she didn't know who he was.

"Oh, you deserve it all right, my sweet, it's your fault I had to kill the beautiful girl who lived with you. If it was you at home, it would have been you instead. I could have had the pleasure of cutting you up instead the voice said."

She felt a knife at her throat, slightly more pressure, and then she could feel a small trickle of liquid running down her neck. Another second and the elevator door opened, Jeremy saw the man holding Ayden and came running towards them.

"What the hell is going on, get your hands off her" he yelled. As he did, the man threw Ayden to the ground, Jeremy figure Ayden was alright and began running after her attacker. Suddenly Jeremy heard Ayden's voice "Jeremy, Jeremy, please stop and come back." Ayden screamed. Jeremy turned and ran back to her as he got to her side, he asked her what was wrong,

"Please open the door and put all the frozen foods in the freezer and the other stuff in the refrigerator." she said.

"Surely this could wait, I almost had him," said Jeremy.

"No, it can't, hurry, quickly"

"What is the rush, oh now I see, why didn't you tell me," Said Jeremy.

"Because you didn't have what I need, great here they come."

"Ayden McKinney the EMY asked. Must be you on the floor."

Ayden quickly said, "I'm twenty-three, one thirty pounds, blood type is o negative, card in my wallet from the Red Cross. I've just been stabbed by some lunatic in the side, happened about five minutes ago, loosing a lot of blood. Better have them hang two bags of blood or I'll be dead soon". Ayden kept closing her eyes but the one taking care of her kept trying to keep her awake.

"What hospital are you taking me to" asked Ayden.

"The closes one, now stay with me, come on focus on my voice," said the man.

"Jeremy, call Michael, tell him what happened and where they are taking me" then she passed out.

They got her out and into the ambulance and got to the hospital within minutes, the man holding her hand thought he lost her pulse. "Hurry guys were losing her" he said.

Chapter Fifteen

"A hysterical Michael running down the hall yelling, where is she, where is she, Jeremy, where is she?"

Jeremy answered that they had her in surgery, that it was bad, that is the most obstinate girl I have ever met, damn her. She makes me put groceries away while she is bleeding lying in the hall. God damn her, I know I could have done something to help her instead of putting ice cream away.

"She is one for the books", said Michael as he continued to pace up and down the hallways. When they finally brought her back and into a room in intensive care, the nurses asked them to leave while they finish prepping her. Michael kept asking questions while Jeremy tried pulling him out.

"Damn it Michael, they told us to leave, come on, it's going to be awhile. Hate to say it but she really looks bad".

"Don't say that she will be fine, she's tough," said Michael." I can't lose her," Michael said to Jeremy with tears in his eyes.

A nurse came out and told them to go to the waiting room downstairs or go home, they couldn't see her tonight.

Ayden lay unconscious for two days, the doctor said it was not uncommon for a patient to be this way after an incident like she had been through.

Jeremy told Michael that they should bring in Miela to see Ayden.

"I bet she would wake up if she felt that dog," said Jeremy.

"How are we going to sneak a dog in here, "replied Michael.

Chapter Sixteen

Michael was pacing thru all the rooms when Jeremy rang that he was parked outside.

"What took you so long" asked Michael.

"Come on buddy relax, it's only seven thirty, and they probably won't let you see her yet. Isn't this the time the shift changes and they change everything and work their magic? replied Jeremy.

"Yes, but I need to get Meila out and fed, don't forget that poor dog has been in that room since early last night. Somehow, they did manage to sneak Miela into Ayden's room.

"Don't you think she might need some relief, if Ayden finds out that dog is neglected, it's trouble with a big T."

"Yea, I forgot about the dog, best not let that slip or we really are in trouble."

"Thank you, now let us get moving, I don't know if I should get her a hamburger or wait to see if she is hungry," added Michael.

"Wait until you see her, maybe she will let someone else take her out," said Jeremy.

"Not in a million years would that dog leave Ayden, I think she would burst before leaving her, that's why I need to get to her" replied Michael.

They got to the hospital finding a parking space close to the main entrance, made their way up to the secure intensive care section. Michael opened the door and was ready for someone to tell him to get out that it wasn't visiting hours, but when a nurse started coming his way, he quickly explained that he was here for the dog. Expecting to get orders to get that big dog out of Ayden's room, Michael was surprised when the nurse didn't say anything.

"Thank heaven you showed up, that poor dog has been circling the bed, we knew it must have to go out, but it wouldn't come to any one. Thanks for being so early, by the time you get back we should have Ayden all cleaned up, so take your time and get that dog some food."

"That's the plan," replied Michael, "any chance Ayden has improved?"

"I'm afraid not honey, not a peep out of her, Doctor said he would be here around ten, so you have plenty of time to give that dog some good exercise., said the nurse."

She led Michael to Ayden's room waited for a reaction from the dog, it was positive, so she opened the door and retrieved the leash, Meila was so happy to see Michael, she cried and licked his face when he put her leash on.

"Hush Meila we don't want to wake Ayden, come on and we will go for a nice walk and some food, and all will be well, well almost well, we still have to find out who did this to her, come on now. Meila pulled Michael; she knew what she needed. She ran right out the back emergency entrance where he had taken her the night before. She wandered this way and that and finally found a place to let her bladder empty. Since they had so much time, Michael just let her go wherever she wanted. Michael thought it was funny that she seemed to be trying to pick up a scent rather then go about her business. Eventually she was back on track, found a place out of sight of most people and completed her job. "She felt so much better" said Michael to Jeremy. Now let's get her something to eat. Jeremy went into the cafeteria and brought back three burgers. Meila had no banner on her to identify her as a special needs dog so she could not really go inside. She waited circling Michael. Finally, Jeremy came out with the food and Meila couldn't wait to get her mouth around some thing, any thing that was in that bag she knew it was for her and before she was done, she ate thru the bag to make sure she got every little piece. She ate the bun, the burgers and the lettuce and tomato's. Jeremy brought a plastic dish and a bottle of water and could not believe how fast that dog lapped up that bottle of water. She gave herself a good shake and Michael knew she wanted to walk some more. He obliged her. They walked and walked but Michael called a halt to the trip because it was nearing ten o'clock. He explained to Meila who looked like she knew what he was talking about when she turned herself around and headed back towards the hospital.

"Is that dog a real one or some kind of built one," asked Jeremy? I never met a dog who looks like she knows what you mean when you tell her what you have to do,"

"I know, it's amazing," answered Michael.

Meila never missed a turn in the street or when she got back to the hospital. One of the nurses saw them coming and Michael explained that he forgot to put her therapy dog vest on. The nurse just smiled and opened the door for him, and Miela went directly to Ayden room. She smelled everything new making sure there was nothing harmful. She reached up and gave Ayden a kiss then lay back down in her usual spot, exhausted from her trip, she cleaned her paws and groomed the rest of herself.

"I wish I had some nurses who were that through with cleaning." The nurse laughed.

Michael took hold of Ayden's hand she was surprisingly warm. He asked if she had a fever but was told no, that she was fine.

"Has the Doctor said any thing at all about her, most importantly if he could comment on when she might wakeup" asked Michael.

"Nope, all we get is our orders on her meds, the room, making sure we move her arms and legs, so she stays strong and watch for any change in attitude from her dog." answered the nurse.

"Has there been any changes in Meila," asked Jeremy?

"Funny you should ask, that very first night she was moved in here a doctor, at least he said he was a doctor, came to the door and asked to see her, the dog went berserk, charging the door, scared the little man so he ran out of here like a streak. Don't think we'll see him again soon, which is fine, the less people coming in here makes writing up reports for the day and extra long time," replied the nurse.

"Jeremy is taking me to work then he will be back to sit with her and occasionally walk Meila," said Michael.

"That's fine, he just has to move out when it's time to change and bath her, I don't know whose little girl she is but only the finest is ordered for her."

"She is indeed special, you will see that when she awakens, answered Michael. "Well Jeremy all is taken care of so now would be a good time to transport me to work, if you please".

"Yes sir" answered Jeremy, "anything you need me to do while you are at work?"

"No," replied Michael, "pick me up please around four oclock, I should be finished by then."

"OK, I'll sit here with Meila and wait to see if anyone comes in," replied Jeremy.

"Thank you, Jeremy, there is no one I rather have with her," said Michael.

After Michael left, and Jeremy sat on the floor next to Meila, the nurse knew Meila's eyes were on her as she finished straightening the room.

"I know you are watching me and if I ever find myself in this kind of situation, I am definitely asking personally for you," she said to Meila. Meila seemed to fully understand and just waged her tail, but you could see that it looked like she was crying, tears running down around her face and her front paws lying over each other. The nurse couldn't stand it, she was told never to act with the dog, but she just couldn't help not watching her so emotional., She picked up a small towel and approached the dog whose eyes were very alert watching the nurse. She began to sit up but didn't feel as if she was in danger, but she was still in the guard position. The nurse tried to talk to her in a soft voice and told her intentions. Jeremy watched the nurse while Meila turned her head back and forth, finally she knew what the nurse was going to do. The nurse took the small towel ran some water over it and gently wiped Meila's face, her eyes especially. It felt so good to Meila, she never bothered to move. When the nurse was finished, she asked Meila if she felt better, and Meila's answer was a nice long lick on her face.

"Good" said the nurse "now we can be buddies, OK." Meila resumed her position on the floor watching the nurse as she left. Meila raised herself and thoroughly and gently circled Ayden's bed.

Finding everything all right she resumed her post position and fell asleep.

"I think you just made a new friend" said Jeremy and watched Meila as she slept.

Chapter Seventeen

"Well I better pick up Michael, or he will be screaming, at me," he said to Miela. I'll be back soon. "Don't let any one in except that nurse who likes you" he said softly to the dog. He knew Miela understood, but the dog was suddenly standing up and gave a small bark. She moved around the bed until she reached Ayden's hand. She licked her hand and moved her nose into her closed hand, Jeremy watched her closely. Miela moaned softly as she continued to move her nose into Ayden's hand. Jeremy watched in amazement as Ayden opened her hand and felt for Miela. The dog was so excited she barked for the first time since Ayden was injured. Ayden opened her eyes, "you silly dog, you know you are not supposed to bark in a hospital."

"I am in the hospital right Jeremy".

"How the hell do you know that" he said.

"Now and then I would wake up, see a nurse hang a new bag of something and you and Michael never made a sound when you were here. I couldn't speak for some reason; my throat wouldn't make a sound, so I stopped trying. I knew if I just stayed quiet it would probably come back."

"Holy shit, oops sorry about that, I am just thinking about Michael," said Jeremy, "I'd better get him", he'll kill me if I knew you were awake and didn't tell him, I'll be right back."

Ayden laughed watching Jeremy gather his stuff and run out the door. He stopped the nurse and told her about Ayden but not to talk to her," Michael would kill us if we were first to hear her voice before him. I'm getting him now ok" and he flew out the door. Michael was waiting at the curb for Jeremy. He got in as quickly as he could; he wasn't even waiting for Jeremy to open the door these days.

"Were you with her all day, did she wake up, did anyone come in, did you see the Doctor," asked Michael.

"No", answered Jeremy one more time. "Only the nurse to change her and to hanging another bottle, that's it."

'I can't wait to see her" said Michael,

"Ok, I'll take Miela out for a walk".

"Thank you, Jeremy, you are such a good friend"

Michael quietly opened the door and Meila came to him, which was strange because she never really liked Michael. With Michael so engrossed in hearing Ayden speak, Michael never noticed how glad Jeremy was to get out and leave him alone with Ayden. He would take a long walk with Miela. He really cared for them both, but a person needs some space. Especially Jeremy, who liked being alone most of the time, got that from Seal training. Ayden was like that he felt, she liked being alone and quiet, Jeremy didn't think the match between Michael and Ayden would make it, Michael was too motherly, and Ayden didn't need that, she was strong on her own.

Jeremy ran into Detective Hildebrant as he was going out the back entrance.

"Any change in Ayden's condition" he asked.

"Yes, it's amazing, Meila went to her and softly moaned and it was magical, Ayden felt around for the dog and spoke to her, Doctor said it could be tomorrow or next month, just proves they don't know everything." replied Jeremy.

"Well, that's about the best news I've had today, good for her".

"Listen, there are some Detectives from some other countries where there have been murders like ours. I would really like for you and Michael to meet them; we have formed a little task force of our own with the OK from the Chiefs. More people with like information could be useful. We have a room in the Manhattan main building, our eyes only, but you would be welcome. We are meeting tonight around seven o'clock, if you and Michael could make it, I know everyone would like to hear Ayden's story. Give Michael the message and hope to see you both tonight". said Hildebrandt.

"Ok, I'll ask Michael".

Chapter Eighteen

Michael was hesitant about leaving Ayden, but Jeremy told him how important this really could be to all the other Detectives who came from other Countries just to get as much information they could and solve their own crimes. "Michael, this could go on killing more and more unless together we have enough to solve this case, it could be just one little thing one of us has and we could get him."

"All right Jeremy, let's go, but I'm not staying long" replied Michael.

"That's fine," we'll just tell them everything we know and tell them we have to leave because of Ayden and especially for poor Meila that has been in the room all day and she needs a break and has to be, they will understand.

Michael and Jeremy walked into the huge room, beautifully decorated with expensive paneling. Michael thought to him self that they must have quite a budget if all the rooms were like this. Each man had their own boards with information about their cases. As soon as Hildebrant saw Michael and Jeremy he rushed to them and shook their hands. "I'm so glad you could make it, any change in Ayden's condition."

"Yes said Michael," she is awake" and talking thanks to Miela and I'm afraid we will have to leave early, Meila needs to be let outside and fed, she has been with Ayden all day.

"Oh, we understand, that is one devoted dog she has there," said Hildebrant.

"Look let me introduce to the rest of our little task force he said"

All the men came closer, very eager to meet them.

Hildebrant started, "you know me, but for now just call me Steve. This is Colin Price, from our Manhattan squad; Colin was tall, well manicured and related to the commissioner. This is Edmun Sims from England, just five years on the job, but liking every minute. This is Joseph Jeneve of course you must recognize him by his accent, he says he doesn't have one it is us that talk funny, but in France this is the way everyone speaks he says. Well, that's everyone" said Steve. It took a few minutes for everyone to shake hands and find a seat near their boards. Everyone had a picture or two on their boards. Michael and Jeremy were glad to see that there were only a few pictures on Brooklyn's board. When they looked down the line of everyone else's, they couldn't believe Jeneve's board. It was almost completely covered. They looked at each other in disbelief. Joseph looked at them and said, "You see why it is important for us to, as you say" pick each other's brains anything, anything could be help to us.

Michael said, "It's a pleasure to work with you all, I only hope we can be helpful."

Steve began with his board, "as you can see, we don't have too many murders but the ones we have had have been horrible, our killer likes to use a knife and butcher his victims. I believe Edmun from England also has had the same killings, am I right, Edmun.?"

"Yes, Steve we are not used to murders like this, a few people strangled to death or shot but not this, this is really more then we have ever seen. The last one just two days ago a couple was birding, and the woman was looking into the water from the small bridge and spotted a woman floating in the water. She always wore long rubber waders in case she needed to rescue a bird. She quickly ran to the side of the stream and grabbed the floaters hand and pulled her from the stream. She told her husband to call the coppers [that's us]. She looked back at the lady and let out a scream said her husband, so he had to see what was wrong with his wife. As soon as he got there, he had to turn and bring up the lunch he had just eaten. He described the victim as being cut every where like you would butcher a pig or chicken; it was the worse thing he ever saw. He took hold of his wife and tried to pull her away, but she was just so focused on the lady she was crying hysterically. When the coroner finally got there, they managed to move her away. All in all, we have had three victims like that and not a single clue." there was silence for a moment then Steve spoke.

"Not a damn clue any where".

Manhattan's Colin said that his victims were in a similar state, He never saw so many patrolmen lose their lunches coming upon a woman butchered like that.

Before Colin could say any thing more, Jeneve jumped in with a handful of pictures like he had on his board and threw them on the table towards the men.

"Here he said before you all cry about the three or four you have, look at this. For a year I see the faces of these women, half of them not even women, too young, much too young and no clues, nothing. I need help much help. Here lay sixteen butchered women. Colin and Edmun both looked as if they were going to lose it, but they held on. There was silence for a few minutes then everyone got up and walked past the different boards. Some one said that they all look the same. Colin agreed long brown hair, lots of makeup on and the lipstick from ear to ear with the same cut.

"I'd like to show the commissioner these photos, maybe we can get more men to patrol, if we get him, he probably is the same one doing this in all the countries, agreed", asked Colin.

Everyone agreed. Colin went to find the Commissioner. The commissioner was reluctant to come but after he walked up and down studying the pictures, his face took on a white look.

"This is the worse I have ever seen in my thirty-one years in blue. Of course, I will personally pick out the men in blue that I know are some of the best when it comes to deviant murders. This was good thinking Colin, let's get this bastard in all the countries, even if we must go there, right men. A chorus of voices could be heard out on the street. "YES SIR."

Chapter Nineteen

All the men took out their phones and began to call their wives or girlfriends or their other partners. They all said about the same, "just a few more days and I'll be home. We're close to getting this guy, yea love you to, bye."

Now what, they stood around looking at each other. "OK, where do we start," said one of them.

"I don't know but before I can do anything I need to get some thing in my stomach, we have been at this all day. A cup of coffee and a bagel just doesn't do it for me, I can't think" said Jeneve. "It is no wonder you are all so thin, food we must have food to keep our brains energized and our bodies ready to go."

It was already early afternoon, just then the phone rang, someone yelled out, no, no it better not be another one. Hildebrant answered the phone Detective Hildebrant speaking, "who, yes of course I remember you, how are you doing" he asked.

"I'm great, could be better, but for now I'm the best I can be." she answered." Look I know it is rather late but I'm sure you are all probably tired of eating from brown paper bags or Chinese containers so how about a home cooked meal, I'll admit I didn't cook it all, but it's really good so how about it." said Ayden.

"Ayden, you just got out of the hospital and those few days you spent on Long Island at Dimitri's house really hasn't given you enough time to heal thoroughly, you should be resting. another few days at least", said Hildebrant.

Michael and Jeremy had spoken to the detective about Ayden, and all of them were concerned that whoever was after her may try again. They agreed that they needed to find a place where she would be safe.

"I think I know a place, but I need to speak to Dimitri first," said Michael.

It was all arranged; they would take Ayden to the Heliport and fly her out to Dimitri's estate on long island and stay with her until they felt she was fully recovered and out of danger. Jeremy was happy to be out of the city, he only stayed because of Michael. He knew he could find a job anywhere else but Michael was to good to him and he felt it wasn't the right time to leave him.

Dimitri's estate was more like a castle than a home. Thick walls surrounded the entire perimeter and to get in you had to pass through the locked gate by calling on the phone. The estate manager was the one who answered and gave permission. Luckly the helicopter had a place to land and everyone was glad that they were finally on the ground. The estate manager was there to greet them and introduced himself to them.

"I hope you had a pleasant ride," he said. "We have a small refreshment waiting for you on the patio, I am Mr. Dimitri's estate manager, if you need anything please don't hesitate to ask. I am Mr. Romanyolo, but every one calls me Rommy as I hope you will to. I will introduce you to the rest of he staff after you have settled in, now if you would please follow me. I'll have your things brought up to the villa."

The days she spent at Dimitrie's were wonderful, but just resting was not for Ayden. If it wasn't for the grounds keeper who let her help him do some weeding and even allowed her to pick some of the flowers to bring inside to brighten up the place a little and especially the woman who maintained the dogs that patrolled the huge yard all the time even at night. She would have gone insane. The place was so quiet, walls all around the place, a house that looked more like a castle than a home and felt like one to. This was no place she wanted to spend more time than she had to. Ayden knew they were just trying to protect her from the nut case that killed Betty and almost killed her, but she just could not feel safe anywhere. Only when she met Meila one of the dogs that patrolled the property, did she feel like things were normal. For some reason she nor the dog keeper understood the bond that Miela and Ayden made with each other. Ayden knew that somehow, she would have to have Miela for her own. She explained the way she felt with Michael and Jeremy but she really never felt safe until she was with Miela. She begged Michael to ask Dimitri if he would be willing to let him buy the dog for Ayden considering the fragile state she was in. Michael said he would pay what ever it cost to make Ayden feel safe. Michael really didn't like dogs much, but he would do anything for Ayden. As it turned out, Dimitri agreed to do this for Ayden.

The dogs patrolled day and night, three during the day and three at night. On the fourth night they were there, Meila who was now sleeping in Ayden's room got up and began barking and scratching at the glass door that led to a small outside porch. Ayden got up and parted the curtain to see what Miela was barking at and saw a man on the steps of the porch. Ayden screamed and Michael and Jeremy who had rooms on either side of her came running in. Ayden told them that there was a man on the porch. Jeremy told Michael to stay with Ayden and to take her down to the small dining room by the kitchen., then Jeremy was out the door.

Michael saw someone in the kitchen and asked if he could make Ayden a cup of hot tea. The two stayed and waited for Jeremy. Hours seemed to go by but Jeremy finally got back.

"Did you see him," asked Ayden.

"Yeah," I chased him but he climbed up a ladder on the west side of the house and got away, he had a car waiting there. I couldn't get a very good look at him, but he was not a very big man, and he moved really fast. Michael called Dimitri the next day to tell him of the events of the night before. Demitri told him not to worry that he would have Mrs. Heigle the woman who kept the dogs to increase the number of dogs that were on patrol at night. He told him that he would be there himself tomorrow to see what they could do to make sure nothing like this would happen again.

Michael relayed what Dimitri told him and Ayden said she still didn't feel safe. If someone wanted her dead, maybe he would continue until he killed her.

Michael yelled at her, "no one in this world could take you away from me, if I have to kill them myself and have no doubt, I would."

"Michael please, calm down I know this isn't your fault and I love you for all you are doing for me," answered Ayden. "You and Jeremy and Meila are all I need."

Mrs. Heigle came out that afternoon and asked everyone to come outside.

"These are new dogs that I have been training, and I would like them to walk among you to get your scent. Please stand still and don't try to pet them or look at them directly in the eyes. They will be patrolling at night and if you should be outside for any reason they should know that you belong here, and will not hurt you. However, they are new and young and not fully trained so if you can avoid going out at night it would be good. Now I will let them walk around you, please stay still. The dogs, half of them Dobermans and half rottweilers walked and sniffed each person then went back to Mrs. Heigle and sat down."

"Very good boys," she said to them and gave them an order to return to their cribs. Each dog immediately ran off as she said.

"Thank you I think they will work out fine, Please feel more secure now," she said and left.

"Well that was something," Said Jeremy. "I know I feel good, how about you guys?"

"I think I just want to go home," said Ayden. "This place reminds me of a prison and not a comfortable place to recuperate."

"If that's what you want Ayden then that is what we will do," replied Michael. "I to don't feel comfortable here."

When Dimitri arrived and they had finished dinner Michael told him that they appreciated all he did for them but Ayden feels that she would like to go back to the city and stay in the apartment with Jeremy. I can always get another car to drive me to work. With Jeremy and Miela she will rest better.

Dimitri said he would do as they asked and said he would have a chopper there for them tomorrow to take them back to the city and he was sorry for the scare that Ayden suffered while she was at his place. Ayden thanked him for everything and told him she couldn't wait until they found this lunatic so she and he could get back to work.

"You know I love you my dear and cannot wait until we are working together again as well." Said Dimitri.

Ayden was back home and everything was perfect. She heard about the task force and wanted to do something to show her appreciation for all the sacrifices they were making trying to catch this killer.

She called Detective Hilderbrant and invited him and the whole task force to the apartment.

"No, I've rested long enough, Please, come to the house" begged Ayden, "I would very much like to meet the whole task force." "Let me ask the boys," "Ayden would like us all to their house for home cooked food, what say you all. Thanks Ayden, they are already out the door, see you soon."

With six of them standing around the table drinking beer and eating little snacks they were all finally relaxed, it was so good for Michael and Jeremy. It was such a surprise for Michael to see his mother and Ayden back by Michael's desk. "I wonder how she pulled this one off" thought Michael, but he didn't care it was just great that they were together. Michael watched Ayden as she removed bottles from the table and set everyone up with another round.

"Who's for salad, pull up a chair because then we have the pasta dish and meatballs followed by cheesecake, coffee and canola's. We can't let you all out with beer bellies, don't know where the Commissioner is tonight." Every one of them laughed. Even Michael and Jeremy were laughing, Ayden was so grateful that Michael's mother thought it was a good idea. Ayden knew she would do anything for Michael. All the men around the table slurping their pasta and devouring the meatballs it really was too funny. Pasta gone, meatballs gone, even last of the salad gone, Mrs. D as they affectionally called her felt so good, she loved cooking for a lot of people; she remembers it just like it was home in Italy.

"You know they didn't leave us anything", she said to her.

"Don't worry, I make some thing good for us." she replied. "Look, look at Michael and Jeremy, they are having such fun, this is how I want Michael to have a life like this. I don't even think he knows he is having fun."

"I think you're right" replied Ayden.

All the men leaned back in their chairs patting their stomachs and thanked Mrs. D for such a wonderful meal.

"No, no, Ayden helped a great deal too" answered Mrs. D.

Michael couldn't be any happier seeing his mother and Ayden working so well together.

The men started to help to clear the table, but Mrs. D said no this was woman's work. They must have more important things to do, like solving this puzzle for one. No woman should have to go thru such a horrible thing. Each man took a chair and others on the couch and theories were thrown about when the doorbell rang. Mrs. D started for the door when Michael stopped her. He told her he wasn't expecting anyone else. Everyone was looking towards the door as Michael slowly opened it.

<h1 style="text-align:center">Chapter Twenty</h1>

Ever one was so surprised when they saw who it was.

"Dimitri, come in please, how about some coffee and a canola, I'm afraid we ate all the pasta, but I bet Mama could make some thing for you", said Michael. Do You need to speak with Ayden?, she is on dishwashing duty but I'll call her for you."

"No I'm not here for Ayden, it is exactly all of you that I have come to speak to." because Hildebrant knew Dimitri somewhat, he got up and offered his chair to him, Dimitri thanked him then wiped his face with his hankerchief.

"On second thought, if you have any coffee left, I could use one" he said, Mrs. D quickly brought him one, sugar and cream on the side.

"Thank you, thank you" he said. "Michael please one moment" He spoke to Michael very softly then Michael went into the kitchen and spoke to Ayden and his mother. They walked thru the living room and around the rest of the men and into Ayden's room wondering what was going on.

"It must be important. Some police work or some thing or Michael wouldn't Have asked us to leave the room" said Mrs. D.

"I think you're right; Michael doesn't usually hide things from me," replied Ayden. "What ever this is it must be pretty important".

"Gentlemen, please sit, before we get started would anyone like more coffee or water or something, this will take longer than a few minutes" said Dimitri.

Everyone got settled in and couldn't wait for Dimitri to speak. They all knew that Steve knew him and that Ayden worked for him and that Michael did the books for the company, so now they will get to know the man himself. He was very imposing, Hair that was fairly long and grey. He carried himself as though he was extremely important. He spoke with a very strong Greek accent, but he was easily understood.

"You are all wondering what I am doing here, yes. It is most important I assure you. Ayden and Michael have known me for many years now and they can tell you that I speak only important things, I have no time to prattle on, so let us begin". Dimitri took of his heavy suede coat and threw it on a chair. He asked Michael for a glass of water took a sip and said he was ready to begin. "You all are here because there have been brutal murders in your countries, am I correct," said Dimitri. He looked around the room noting that everyone said yes very softly.

"OK then, let us not beat around the bushes as they say. I know a person who likes to cut things, people, especially women with long brown hair. He loves them, takes them to dinner at the finest places, and buys the finest champagne. Takes them dancing if that is what they like. Whatever they like, he provides. He is a small man, one you would not notice if you passed him on the street, always impeccably dressed. In a group of people, he always acts extremely shy. He doesn't stand out; he just blends into the background. There are only two things that makes him noticeable, One is the foreign purple sports car and the other is his hat and suit that he loves to wear. One that looks slightly purple or lavender some would call it. I have seen his work when Detective Hildebrant asked us to come to Brooklyn to see his work there. I will never, never forget what that poor woman looked like when he was through. I don't think any of us ever will. So, back to the man who inflected all the cuts on the woman. Who of you have had cases like this, where the women were cut most cruelly?" A few men raised their glasses and agreed it was horrible, never had they ever seen such a thing.

"Yes, now you know of what I speak. A monster, yes a monster brought up in a good home, given the best education, best clothes, travel around the world, given money to travel back and forth between here and Europe, speaks English, French and Italian. You would say that he was some lucky man, yes?, So many people would love to be in his shoes, but still he is not satisfied. Something is missing he would say. His mother and I would ask him, what else we can provide for you to make you happy. Finally, the other evening while we dined, he told me what he is doing that makes him so happy. I was at first appalled, then he laughed and so did I knowing he was just kidding with me. But something in his laugh, something in the way he held his head, something about everything didn't sit right. His laugh gave me the chills; he gave me a look that I cannot forget seeing. Gentle men you must think I have gone out of my mind but after a little more conversation, I know I am right. I give to you, and it breaks my heart but this cannot go on, my son, Gregor Tsoukalas. I have flown to Greece to see his mother; I have gone to Paris to speak with people who I believe tell me the truth. I have gone over the calendar to check dates when he is supposed to be in a certain place, but he is not. I have caught him in so many lies, and Ayden who I love like a daughter came to me herself knowing how much I would believe her and knowing how much I love my son, that he is the one who tried to kill her on two different occasions, he kills and destroys of this I have no doubt. So please, believe me when I tell you without a doubt this is the butcher, the monster who takes such pleasure in mutilating these women."

Dimitri stood before them bent over trying to stop the tears from running down his face.

You must get him now before he kills again or leaves the country and kills some where else where it will be harder to find him; he has many places to hide and he knows evil people who would hide him.

Steve, Edmun, Colin and Jeneve as well as the Commissioner all looked around at each other.

"You are absolutely sure" asked Steve, "because in the little time I've known her, I believe in Ayden. She is not the kind of person who would make up something like that."

"I believe her completely, with all my heart, she only tells the truth" replied Dimitri.

"Commisioner", asked Colin, "do you think we have enough proof to try him?"

"Well on just his father's word and Ayden's it will be very difficult, if we only had something more."

"We have" said Dimitri, "Gregor has a locked box with all kinds of ribbons and jewelry taken from the women he killed. I know this because He showed them to me. He thought I really didn't believe him; they are in a drawer in his tall dresser. If you can get a warrant to search his place you would find the box and match them to any of the women he murdered."

"That would do it here", said the Commissioner, "but if he is as clever as they say, how do we get him without warning him first".

"I know I must sound like a father who hates his son, but believe me, I love him more then you can know, but one day he will be killed, by a policeman or by a woman's lover and maybe tortured like he does the women. They say people like him get killed one way or another, but killed by a homemade knife in prison sounds better then being knifed on the streets of Paris." said Dimitri. "If you will allow me one more minute," he said, "I have a plan, I think of it every day, I try not to but I can not help it, another woman dead on my conscious and I think I could not handle any more."

"We cannot imagine how you must be suffering through this," said the Commissioner. "Please go on Dimitri."

"When Gregor is in Manhattan, we always try to have dinner together, I like to cook, as does Gregor so we make something we both like and cook in my apartment. When he was five or six he would like to peel potatoes or carrots, he learned at an early age how to use a peeler. So, when I know I will be having an early day off, I call him and if he is free we decide what to eat. I shop once I leave work and start to prepare the meal. Gregor comes in well before I am done; he also still likes to cut the vegetables. When dinner is finished, we sit with a good bottle of wine and talk about usual things a father and son talk about, well not so usual for this father and son. We have coffee and desserts and clean up and he helps with the dishes, sounds like a good son, no. We hug goodbye and he usually leaves around eleven o'clock. If you could post your men some at the front and some at the rear of the building, but they must be very careful not to be seen, Gregor gets up many times during dinner to look out the windows, if any one is seen he will leave immediately, he is that paranoid. If all goes well, you can grab him when he leaves after dinner if you have a warrant to search his place, you will find the things during the search. No one must know I have told you this or his lawyer or court will dismiss everything, and I will have lost the faith of my son and we will never get the chance to find him again, and no doubt he will kill me or have one of his people do it for him and here I do not lie. Do you think this is a good plan, Commissioner?" asked Dimitri.

"Yes, it's good, and none of this leaves this room got it, YOU GOT IT, if I find out that any one has let any part of the plan out of the bag, he better start looking for new job." said the Commissioner pounding his fist on the table. You gents from England or France please don't phone home until we have him in our custody, agreed". Everyone agreed with the Commissioner.

"You all will play a part if you want to".

"Mr. Tsoukalos, We can not thank you for every thing you are doing to help us. There are no words I can find for the strength in your character and for the pain you must be going through. Please call me the moment you are ready to have dinner and God willing no one gets hurt especially Gregor."

Chapter Twenty-one

Everything went off as it was planned, except no one told the sniper on the roof that Gregor was to be taken alive, and this sniper never missed his target, by the time Detective Hildebrant got to Demitri's apartment one shot was heard. The Detective hesitated before he opened the door. He opened it, took his handkerchief from his pocket, closed the door, rested his back against the wall and cried. Not everything always goes as planned. When he walked into the room, he found Dimitri on the floor holding his son.

"I'm so sorry" said the Detective, "the sniper on the roof across the street said his orders were to take the son down, I'm not sure how he got those orders, but I will find out."

"No, do not worry about the sniper, it was bound to happen some time. Maybe it is better this way, with my son's luck, he could get off on a technicality if he went to court. So this is better, over and done with all cases closed and no more women getting butchered. I prayed for him every night but I think this is Gods answer for us. Please thank everyone who gave so much of their time away from their families, without them who knows how long this would go on. I myself will get back to my business and wait for the return of my best employee Ayden, hoping she will return. She is the only one who can save my sanity. She is the daughter I always wished for."

"Yes said the detective, she is one in a million, I don't know where she got her strength or her smarts but you are right to hope she comes back to work but I think she will need some time to recuperate"

"Yes" replied Demitri, "she deserves as much time as she needs".

Chapter Twenty-Two

It was about three weeks since Gregor was shot, every one still Seemed in shock. They all went about their business but you could tell that something wasn't right. You could feel it in everything you did. Ayden wondered how long it would take for everything to get back to the real normal and not this some where out of the real normal. Even Miela knew things were not right in this house. Everyone did what they usually did but something wasn't right causing the dog to whine now and then. Ayden Wondered what if Gregor wasn't dead would they have taken him back to France to face the charges there. How many murders would he be charged With. Michael said probably thirteen but it could go as high as Eighteen depending on how much evidence they had for each murder. He would probably get the death sentence and what was the death sentence in France.

No one seemed to know, perhaps it was better that she didn't know.

Ayden decided that sitting in the apartment every day was not helping her get over the last few months, so she decided to go back to work.

Michael and Jeremy thought it was a good idea getting around people and the business of creating her designs. She knew Dimitri was not supposed to be in the office until next week so she would have time to regain her routine and to get thing back to normal, what ever that was. She wasn't sure anymore if things would ever be back to normal.

She arrived back to work on Thursday morning expecting a quiet day. All to soon she knew she was wrong. The cutters and sewers were all working, but she had been gone so long she hadn't a clue about what they were working on. She didn't recognize any of the work they were doing. Dimitri must have designed a new clothing line. She got to the second floor and was greeted by Dimitri's sectary, she looked stunned when she saw Ayden.

"Good morning Sylvia," she said to the woman who looked pale and confused.

"Are you coming back to work Ayden," asked Sylvia "Please tell me you are coming back. It is so bad here, the whole place is falling apart."

"But I saw all the people working the sewers must be working a new line, has Dimitri started a new line?"

"We don't know what we're doing, one day he turns up and has people doing one thing and the next day he has everyone doing sone thing else. I don't know what's wrong with him. He is just not the same."

"Well, he did just loose his son. I guess he hasn't gotten over it yet," said Ayden. "Maybe he left a note on my desk telling me what we should be working on."

There was a letter on her desk and as she read it she Started to cry. She knew she needed Michael and Jeremy. She called Jeremy and asked him where Michael was that day and if he could contact him and bring him to the factory, she said it was important and she was afraid.

Michael and Jeremy arrived an hour later and immediately Went to Ayden's office. Michael spoke first asking Ayden what was going on that was so important. Ayden gave Michael the letter and he just stood there reading it again and again, then he finally handed it to Jeremy and sat down.

Jeremy read the letter and he to looked stunned.

"I'm sure he doesn't mean this Ayden," said Jeremy.

"Unfortunately, I think he does. Everyone here says the last few weeks he just comes and goes. It's the last part I'm really worried about."

The letter stated that everything he owned he was leaving to Ayden. He wrote down the name of the lawyer she was to contact, and he would explain everything. He planned his own funeral and that he meant to take his own life. He wrote that he couldn't live any longer with the death of Gregor which he said was all his fault. He couldn't live with the guilt. He hoped she would forgive him because he loved her as is own and couldn't bear it if she couldn't forgive him. My love for you is everything, and I only hope that Michael and Jeremy will always be there for you. My love Goodbye.

"You don't think he really plans to take his own life, do you?" asked Jeremy.

"You read the letter" replied Ayden and I think he already has. Michael would you please call Detective Hildebrant and ask him to send some one to Dimitri's apartment to check.

"Yes, yes right now," answered Michael.

The wait seemed to take forever but eventually the phone rang.

"Michael could you please answer it, I don't think I can."

Michael answered the phone just saying yes, yes and thank you. He turned to Ayden but with the look on his face she knew what he was going to say.

"I'm sorry Ayden, but they found him"

Ayden didn't cry, she calmly gathered her things, told Sylvia to let the staff know that the factory would be closed for the rest of the month, but that everyone would receive their pay. She also told her she would inform her when the details for Dimitri's funeral would be.

"Oh god, I knew something bad was going to happen," she said. "Did He say anything to us?"

"Yes, he said to say goodbye to the best people he ever worked with."

"What about the future," asked Sylvia.

"I have been left everything and as soon as I think I can straighten things out I will decide whether I can do this job without him, because he was a tough man to follow."

"Please take me home Michael, I really need time to process all of this. It looks like my life is about to change and I don't know if I'm ready for it. I really need Meila now more than ever."